The Book
of Me

The School of Life

Published in 2021 by The School of Life
First published in the USA in 2022
70 Marchmont Street, London WC1N 1AB

Illustrations and cover © Ben Javens 2021
Designed and typeset by Marcia Mihotich
Printed in Lithuania by Balto Print

A proportion of this book has appeared online at
www.theschooloflife.com/thebookoflife

The School of Life is a resource for helping us understand
ourselves, for improving our relationships, our careers and our
social lives – as well as for helping us find calm and get more
out of our leisure hours. We do this through creating films,
workshops, books, apps and gifts.

www.theschooloflife.com

ISBN 978-1-912891-61-0

10 9 8 7 6 5 4 3 2 1

Contents

Introduction

What is a Self-Explorer?

An explorer is someone who takes a journey into the unknown. They travel to places where no one has been before – islands, jungles, caves or deserts – in order to learn more about them.

This book is going to help you become an explorer. You'll be going on a journey into uncharted territory, somewhere no one else has ever explored.

→ Before you set off, you'll need to fill out your passport...

Name

....

....

Date of birth

....

Country of birth

....

→ Next, you'll need to pack your suitcase. Draw three of your favourite things in your suitcase to take with you on your journey (we've already packed all the boring things like your clothes and your toothbrush for you).

→ Finally, you'll need to find somewhere comfortable to sit. Here are some suggestions:

You won't be travelling there by boat or plane – indeed, you won't even need to get up from where you're sitting. You'll be going on a **psychological*** journey – which means travelling inside your mind. And you won't be exploring an island, or a jungle. Instead, you'll be exploring your **self**.

On a chair by a window

Under a tree

Curled up on the sofa

Tucked up in bed

(*The word *psychological* is a useful one that we got from the ancient Greeks. *Psyche* means mind and *logos* means study – that is, something related to the study of the mind.)

What is the Self?

Your self is a part of your **mind**. It's not the part that controls digestion, or tells your feet where to go. It's the part that **thinks** and **feels**, that **experiences** the world around you. It's the part that makes you *you*.

It's made up of all sorts of things.

* Your **thoughts**
* Your **emotions**
* Your **beliefs**
* Your **memories**
* Your **conscience** (your sense of right and wrong)
* Your **imagination**
* Your **talents**
* Your **weaknesses**
* Your **hopes and dreams**
* Your **fears and worries**
* Your **memories**

In some religions and cultures, the self is called the **soul**. Some people believe it lives on after death, or that it is reincarnated in a different body.

Why We Need Explorers

Before there were explorers, nobody knew what much of the world looked like. Until we were able to travel vast distances on ships or by plane, people only knew about the places they happened to live in. As a result, maps often used to look like this:

Cartographers (the people who make maps) had to guess what other places looked like. Countries were drawn with the wrong shape and geography – or simply weren't drawn at all. If no one they knew had ever been there, they labelled them *terra incognita* ('unknown places'). Instead of roads, towns or rivers, they drew fantastical creatures, who they imagined must live there – like magicians, or monsters.

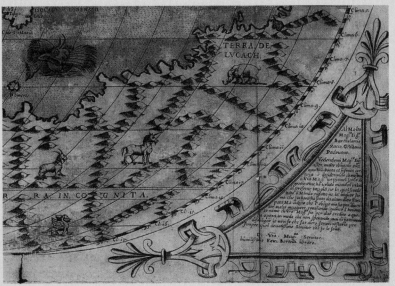

→
Can you name the different types of fantastical creatures?

It took explorers to help us understand what the world really looked like. Explorers like Ferdinand Magellan, James Cook, Isabella Bird and Gertrude Bell set off on long voyages across the sea to discover new countries and continents.

Sometimes, they found things they weren't expecting. The Italian explorer Christopher Columbus sailed west from Spain hoping to find a new sea passage to India... but ended up discovering America instead.

Thanks to explorers, our maps now look like this:

Your self is a lot like an undiscovered country. You might think you know 'you' quite well. But the vast majority of who you are has yet to be discovered. If your self was a map, it would look like this:

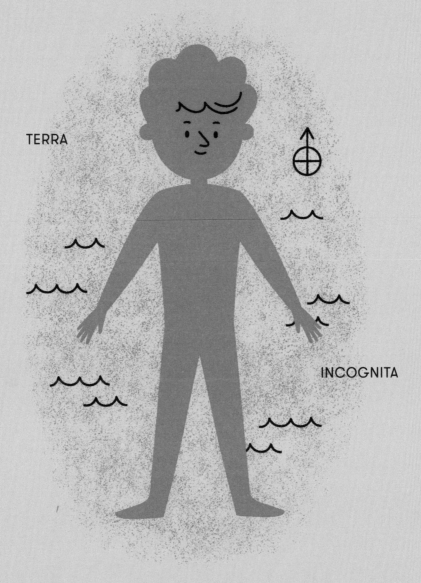

The journey to discover your self will be long. It won't always be easy. There is enough inside you that it could take a whole lifetime to fully explore.

Only You Can Know Yourself

Think about someone you live with (it might be someone in your family, like a parent or grandparent). You probably know quite a lot about them. You might know the colour of their eyes, what they like to have for breakfast, or how hairy their ankles are.

→ Write down five things you know about this person.

1 ....

2 ....

3 ....

4 ....

5 ....

But there's a lot you probably don't know. Most importantly, you don't know exactly what's going on inside their heads – what they are really thinking, or feeling.

Possible mysteries about...

1. What do they dream about?
2. What are they most scared of?
3. What do they think of their childhood?
4. What do they feel sad about at night?
5. What do they regret?

Much of the time, we have to guess what people are thinking using clues drawn from their facial expressions, or the ways they behave.

→ Try this now. Guess what each of these people is thinking and feeling.

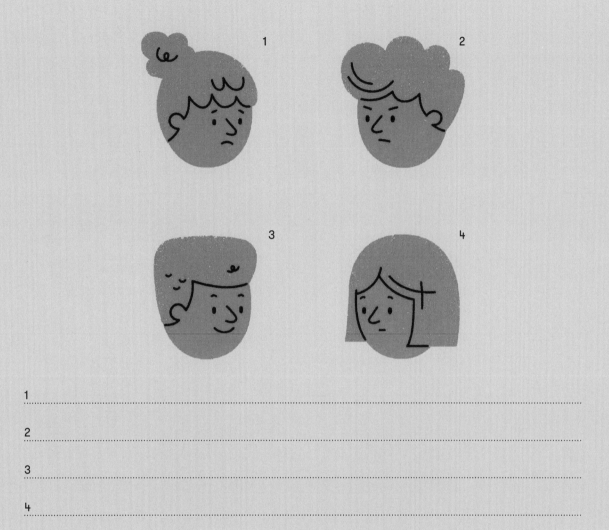

1 ....

2 ....

3 ....

4 ....

People might tell you some of the things they think and feel (by saying things like "I'm in a good mood", "I'm quite cross with you today" or "Not now, I'm very tired") but they won't tell you everything. They might be embarrassed by what they're feeling – or confused about the cause.

The only person you can truly know on the inside is yourself. Only you know what you are really thinking and feeling – which means that only you have the ability to discover who you really are. Knowing ourselves is really hard, but it's a properly exciting task.

Everyone needs to go on journeys of self-exploration, but because they are hard, many of us never get around to it. Sometimes people tell you they are 'too busy' to be self-explorers, but that's likely to be an excuse. They're not too busy; they're too lazy!

Why We Need Self-Knowledge

By exploring the contents of our minds, we can learn things about ourselves we wouldn't otherwise have understood. This is called gaining **self-knowledge**.

Without self-knowledge, we are like cartographers drawing a map of an unknown country:

We won't know what parts of ourselves are really like – such as what our beliefs are, or what we might be worried about.

✳

We'll make mistakes – like making friends we don't actually care for, or choosing a job that doesn't suit us.

✳

We'll think parts of ourselves are strange or dangerous, even though they are actually normal.

✳

We'll tell lies about ourselves to others, because we can't be honest about who we are.

Self-knowledge is useful in all sorts of ways – some of which we'll explore in this book. The more self-knowledge you gain, the better off you'll be.

Gaining self-knowledge isn't easy – in fact, it's one of the most difficult things a person can do. Like explorers, we'll need to be brave and work hard. And we'll need to keep a record of our discoveries by writing things down (or by drawing, or colouring, or sticking things in).

Socrates, a philosopher who lived a long time ago in Greece, said the purpose of life was to:

You might not want to spend ALL your life exploring yourself – but it's probably the most interesting bit of travel you'll ever go on.

Exploring My Mind

Exploring My Mind

Your mind is the part of you that **thinks**. Here are some of the different types of thinking the mind does.

PERCEIVING
Experiencing the world through the senses

IMAGINING
Having new ideas

REASONING
Using logic to work things out

FEELING
Having emotions

COMMUNICATING
Speaking, reading and writing

REMEMBERING
Storing experiences

DESIRING
Wanting things

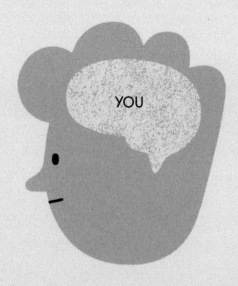

YOU

→ Give some examples of these different types of thinking by completing the following sentences. (You used your mind's ability to **communicate** by completing these sentences)

PERCEIVING: Something I saw today is

....

....

REASONING: Using reason, I know that 2 + 6 =

....

....

FEELING: Something I felt today is

....

....

REMEMBERING: Something I remembered today is

....

....

IMAGINING: Something I imagined today is

....

....

DESIRING: Something I desired today is

....

....

Together, all these different types of thinking make up your mind.

Brain vs Mind

The part of your body responsible for your mind is your **brain**. It's a large, wrinkly organ that lives inside your skull and looks a bit like a big walnut.

We often use the terms 'mind' and 'brain' to mean the same thing. But whereas your brain is a **physical object**, your mind isn't. In this way, your brain/mind is a bit like a computer. The brain is the **hardware** (the casing, circuits and wires) and the mind is the **software** (the programs, videos and games).

→ Can you guess which of these are a part of your **brain** and which are a part of your **mind**? Try to sort them below (and ask an adult to help you if you're not sure).

Synapses   Frontal Lobe

                          Memories

            Nerves   Emotions

Ideas   Cerebellum   Beliefs

Brain	Mind

Brain Maze

If you look at a picture of the brain, you'll notice it's made up of lots of different wrinkles and folds. These folds bring different parts of your brain closer together to help you think faster. Your brain gets more wrinkly over time as you grow (a process called **gyrification**) – and your mind grows bigger and more **complex** along with it.

→ Can you solve this brain maze? Draw a path from the start to the finish.

Start

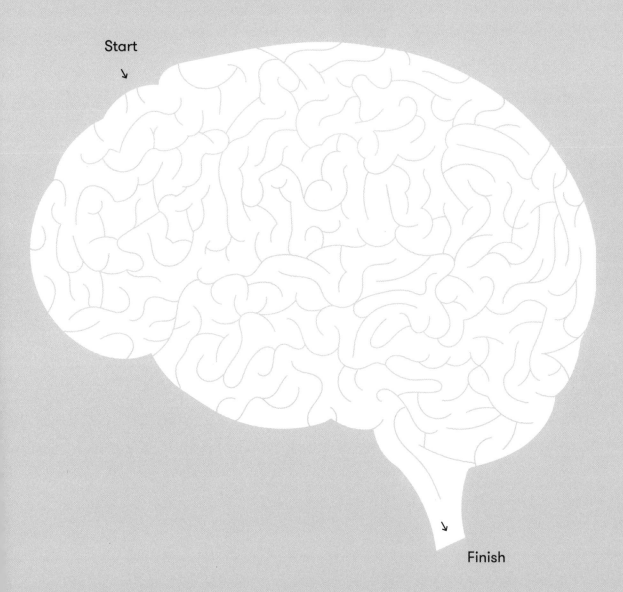

Finish

How Our Minds Work

The human mind is often compared to a computer. Just like a computer it receives **inputs** (from our **body** and through our **senses**) and turns them into **outputs** (as different **behaviours** and **emotions**).

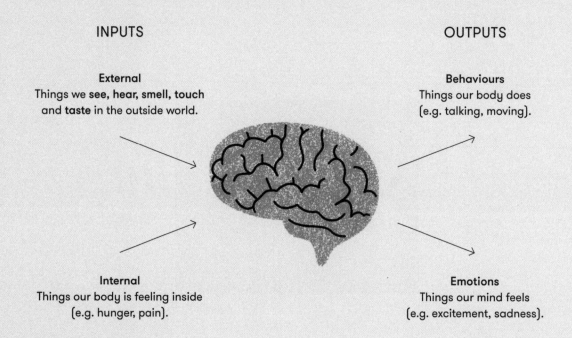

INPUTS

External
Things we **see**, **hear**, **smell**, **touch**
and **taste** in the outside world.

Internal
Things our body is feeling inside
(e.g. hunger, pain).

OUTPUTS

Behaviours
Things our body does
(e.g. talking, moving).

Emotions
Things our mind feels
(e.g. excitement, sadness).

Here's an ice cream based example to show how this works:

INPUTS

Seeing and **hearing** the
ice cream van.

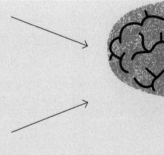

OUTPUTS

Walking to the ice cream van.
Asking to buy an ice cream.

Our body is **feeling hot** and a
bit **hungry.**

Feeling excited to taste the
ice cream.

→ Can you show how your mind works? Following the example above, write down the thoughts that show how inputs are processed to make outputs.

INPUTS

OUTPUTS

External

Behaviours

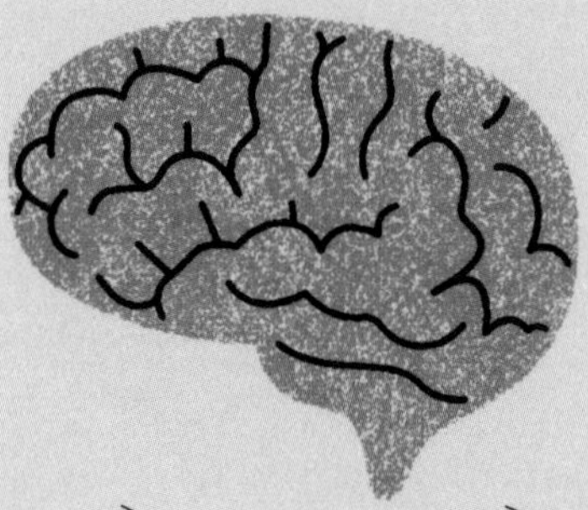

Internal

Emotions

Thought:
"I should put on
a jumper."

INPUTS

OUTPUTS

External

....

....

....

....

Behaviours

....

....

....

....

Thought:
"That old woman
needs help."

Internal

....

....

....

....

Emotions

....

....

....

....

Noisy Minds

From the outside, thinking seems quite simple. In comic books, for example, illustrators use thought bubbles to show what characters are thinking, like so:

But our minds don't work like they do in comic books. We rarely think one thought at a time. Instead, our minds are full of a jumble of different thoughts, all going on at the same time.

Our minds are noisy – so much so that it can be hard to tell exactly what we're thinking at any one time.

This is one reason we need to explore our minds – so we can work out exactly what's inside them.

Stream of Consciousness

To be **conscious** means to be aware of your own thoughts. It means we're able to recognise, say or write what we're thinking.

A stream of consciousness is a type of writing that tries to show the way the mind really works. Rather than try to order thoughts, you write whatever comes into your head.

→ Create your own stream of consciousness. For the next few minutes, write down every single thought that comes into your head, no matter how small (or strange).

Is there anything you wrote that surprised you? Underline it: it might be worth investigating further.

The Unconscious

So far, we've been talking about the **conscious** mind. This is the part we know about.
If someone asks you "what are you thinking?", you will tell them about your conscious
thoughts – the ones you are *aware* of.

But there's a whole other part of our minds that we *aren't* aware of. This is called the
unconscious. It's made up of:

* Unconscious **desires**
* Unconscious **beliefs**
* Unconscious **memories** (those our conscious minds have forgotten)
* Unconscious **fears**

Your mind is a bit like an iceberg. You can see your conscious mind pretty clearly...
but your unconscious mind is hidden.

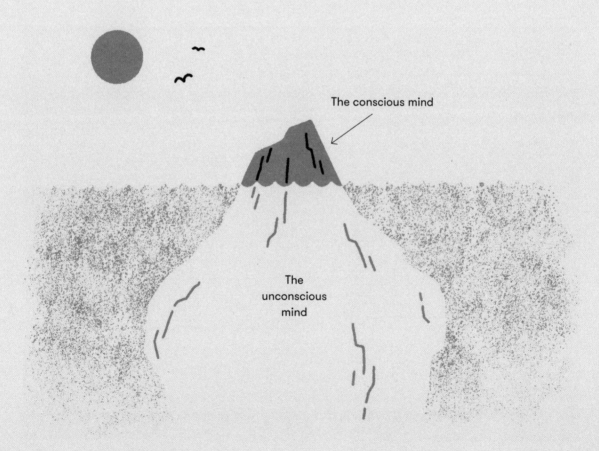

The conscious mind

The
unconscious
mind

Even though our unconscious thoughts are hidden, they can still be very powerful. They can affect the ways we think and behave.

✳ If we spend a lot of time pretending to be a superhero, it might be because we have an **unconscious desire** to be famous and powerful (like a superhero).

✳ If we're unusually shy, it might be because we have an **unconscious belief** that we're unlikable (so we worry people won't like us).

✳ If we're unusually anxious, it might be because we have an **unconscious memory** of something bad happening to us when we were very young (and want to avoid it happening again).

✳ If we find it difficult to sit down and do our homework, it might be because we have an **unconscious fear** of failure (so we don't want to try).

Discovering our unconscious mind is quite difficult. To do so, we might need to practice **therapy** (which we'll learn more about at the end of the chapter).

The Faulty Walnut

Earlier, we explored how in some ways our minds are a bit like computers. But in other ways, they're not like computers at all. In fact, they're very **faulty**, and make a lot of mistakes.

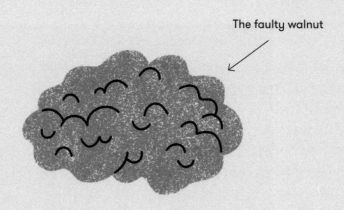

The faulty walnut

They make mistakes about the **inputs.** We might feel like shouting or punching a wall because of an **external** input, like hearing something annoying a teacher has said to us. But actually, it could really be because of an **internal** input, like the fact that we're thirsty, or we've got a stomach ache.

We make mistakes about the **outputs**. If someone is kind to us, we should really respond with kind **behaviour** in return – but for some reason (maybe because of an **unconscious belief** that we don't deserve to be treated kindly) we behave badly, by being rude or making fun of them.

At The School of Life, we like to call the mind the 'faulty walnut', because of all the mistakes it makes. Exploring our minds is important, because it helps us understand the mistakes they make.

My Lizard Brain

One of the reasons our brains are tricky is because of evolution. Humans evolved from more primitive species of animal, like lizards. Over time, the human brain became more complex and capable of reason. But parts of our brains are still very lizard-like. It's useful to think of our brain having two parts – part human, and part reptile.

Our lizard brain controls things like:

* **Aggression** – making us get angry easily
* **Territoriality** – making us protective of our space and belongings
* **Habituality** – making us need a set routine
* **Fear** – making us constantly alert to danger

These things are useful if you're a lizard, but not so much so if you're human. They mean we get angry and scared very easily in situations that don't call for it – like throwing a tantrum when we lose a sock, or being shy when we meet a stranger.

What situations make you angrier than they should?

....

....

....

What situations make you more scared than they should?

....

....

....

Getting scared or angry when we shouldn't is very normal – it's just our lizard brain talking. Remembering this can help us recognise when we're thinking like a lizard, rather than a human.

Mental Illness

Just like our bodies, our minds can sometimes get **ill**. There are different types of mental illness. Some can make us believe things that are untrue and harmful. Others can make us confused as to what is real or what is not.

In the past, people who were mentally unwell were treated very badly. They were labelled 'mad' or 'insane'. The cures they were given mostly didn't work and were often quite cruel.

The truth is, none of us is 'mad'. Anyone can get unwell… and, with the right help, anyone can get better.

Therapy

The best way we have of understanding our minds (and making them work better) is **therapy**. There are lots of different kinds of therapy, but at its heart, it involves **talking to someone else about your thoughts**.

Therapy is useful because we're not very good at understanding our own minds and thoughts. But if we talk to someone else, they can help us see things we might have missed or misunderstood.

Talking about your thoughts can be hard. You might feel embarrassed or ashamed by them, or unsure as to what your thoughts really are, or mean.

There are **professional** therapists who give therapy as part of their job. They can help if you have more serious problems. But you don't need to see an expert to have therapy – all you need is to talk to someone you trust.

If you had to talk to someone about your thoughts, who would you choose?

....

Why would you choose this person?

....

....

....

....

So, whenever you feel particularly worried or confused about your thoughts, the best form of help is to talk about them.

Philosophical Meditation

One of the easiest ways to examine the contents of your mind is by using a technique called philosophical meditation. It involves asking yourself three simple (but very important) questions.

1. What am I currently **worried** about?
2. What am I currently **upset** about?
3. What am I currently **excited** about?

Even though the questions are simple, most people don't take the time to ask them. They don't have a clear idea of what they're thinking and feeling.

→ Set aside 10 minutes and answer the questions.

What are you currently worried about?

....

....

....

....

What are you currently upset about?

....

....

....

....

What are you currently excited about?

....

....

....

....

It's a very good idea to use philosophical meditation as often as possible – we'd recommend once a week as a good target.

My Mind Journey Postcard

Now that you've explored your mind, it's time to fill out your postcard. Use this space to record some of the things you've learned about yourself and your mind in this chapter.

→ On this side, draw and colour in a picture of something you've explored (perhaps a brain, or a computer).

1 ....
....
....

2 ....
....
....

3 ....
....
....

→ On this side, write down the three most
important things you've learned during
the chapter.

Exploring My Moods

When we talk about our mood, we're talking about emotions, or our *feelings*. Here are some examples:

→ How are you feeling right now? Circle the emotion that's closest to how you're feeling.

Anger

Boredom

Loneliness

Happiness

Calm

Sadness

Envy

Fear

Amusement

Guilt

Worry

Disgust

Some emotions are positive – they put us in a good mood. And some are negative – they put us in a bad mood.

→ Which of these emotions are positive or negative? Sort them into this chart:

Positive Emotions	Negative Emotions

Complex Emotions

Emotions are complicated. You might think you know most of them already. There are lots of different ones, some of them with quite long names.

→ See if you can guess what these emotions feel like. Draw a line from each emotion to what you think it might feel like. If you're not sure, ask a grown-up to help you.

1 MELANCHOLY, or feeling MELANCHOLIC

2 NOSTALGIA, or feeling NOSTALGIC

3 APATHY, or feeling APATHETIC

4 HUMILIATION, or feeling HUMILIATED

5 VULNERABILITY, or feeling VULNERABLE

6 REMORSE, or feeling REMORSEFUL

7 ECSTASY, or feeling ECSTATIC

8 ANXIETY, or feeling ANXIOUS

9 SERENITY, or feeling SERENE

10 GRATITUDE, or feeling GRATEFUL

It's useful to have a lot of words to describe the feelings we have. It means that when people ask us how we're feeling, we'll be able to tell them with real accuracy. Knowing how to read words is called literacy; knowing how to read feelings is called emotional literacy.

a Feeling calm and peaceful

b Feeling weak

c Feeling thankful

d Feeling worried

e Feeling really, really, really good

f Feeling like you miss things in the past

g Feeling like you don't care about anything

h Feeling like other people are laughing at you

i Feeling bad about things you've done in the past

j Feeling sad about life in general

What Causes Our Moods?

Most of the time, our moods are caused by our *experiences*. The things we feel are affected by the things that happen to us.

Some experiences make us happy. Some make us sad. Some make us frightened, or angry, or guilty.

→ What do these experiences make you feel? (You can look back at the first page of this chapter for possible clues.)

Winning a running race

....

....

Being stuck inside on rainy day

....

....

Eating a big bag of crisps all in one go

....

....

Losing a sock

....

....

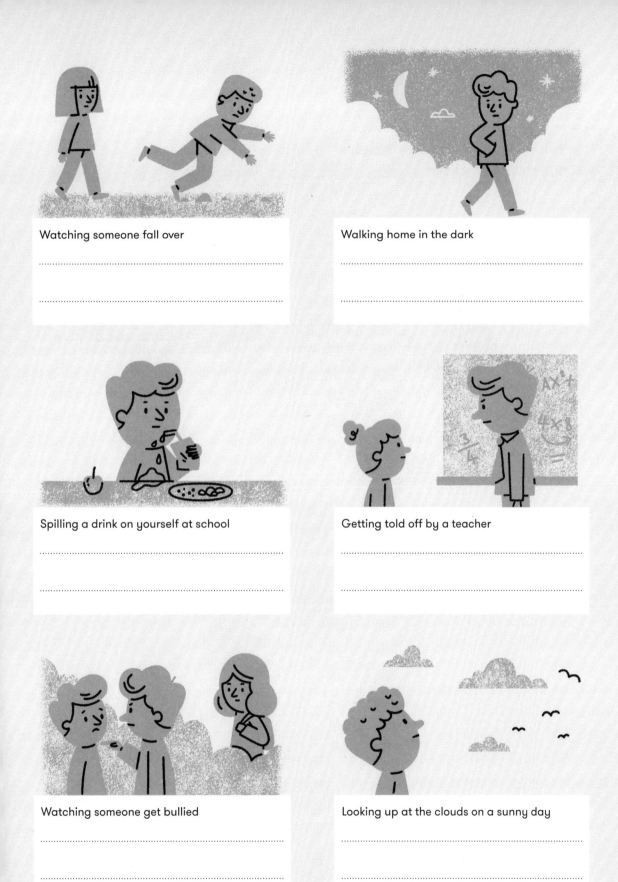

Watching someone fall over

....

....

Walking home in the dark

....

....

Spilling a drink on yourself at school

....

....

Getting told off by a teacher

....

....

Watching someone get bullied

....

....

Looking up at the clouds on a sunny day

....

....

Moods and Behaviour

Emotions are very powerful. They control our behaviour – making us do things, or act, in very different ways.

→ What emotions make you feel like...

Hiding in a cupboard?

....

....

....

Dancing?

....

....

....

Saying mean things?

....

....

....

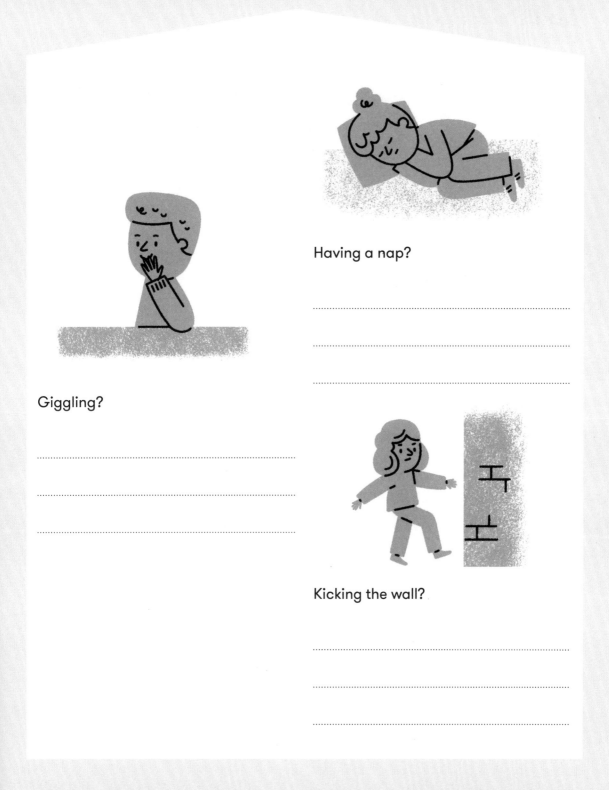

Having a nap?

....

....

Giggling?

....

....

....

Kicking the wall?

....

....

....

When examining your own behaviour, or the behaviour of other people, it's important to think about what emotions may have caused it.

Words

When it comes to our emotions, words matter. Our mood can be strongly affected by things other people say to us – and especially *about* us.

→ In the speech bubbles, write down some words or phrases other people say that put you in a *good* mood – words that make you feel happy, excited and loved.

You're really funny!

I'm very proud of you

It's ice cream for dessert

Well done

→ Now write down some words or phrases that put you in a *bad mood* – words that make you feel sad, angry, embarrassed or upset.

Sometimes, grown-ups say:
"Sticks and stones may break your bones, but words will never hurt you."

But this is WRONG. Words are extremely powerful, and can be very hurtful. Sometimes things people say to us can stay with us for a long time.

Don't be so stupid

You're being so annoying

We can't afford that

Places

Our moods are affected by our environment. Where we are in the world, what time of day it is, and what it's like outside, can influence the way we feel.

One thing that can affect how we feel is the weather. That may sound simple, but it isn't. We often use weather words to describe our emotions. If we're happy, we might say we're in a *sunny* mood, whereas someone who's sad might be described as *dismal* or *gloomy*.

Not everyone feels the same way about the weather. Some people say they feel sad on rainy days, but others say rain makes them feel relaxed and peaceful.

→ Draw your mood as if it were weather. Show how each situation opposite makes you feel by drawing the kind of weather that you feel represents it.

My birthday

Going to the dentist

Losing a video game

Eating too much

Different places can also put us in particular moods. When you're in your bedroom, for example, you might feel safe and calm, but being in your school classroom might make you feel bored, or worried.

→ Above, draw a place that puts you in a *good* mood.

→ Now draw a place that puts you in a *bad* mood.

Of course, our environment isn't the *only* thing that affects our mood. If we're in a particularly good or bad mood, changing our environment won't help very much. But it can be useful to think about what the weather might be doing to our mood – almost without us being aware.

Mood and Body

We've seen how emotions have an effect on our bodies. Certain emotions can make our bodies do different things. When we're excited, we might jump up and down. When we're angry, we might grind our teeth, or shout very loudly.

→ Draw what your body does when you feel...

Excited

Scared

But sometimes this happens the other way around. Our bodies can be the *cause* of our emotions.

→ See if you can answer the following questions:

Being hungry makes me feel

....

....

....

....

Being tired makes me feel

....

....

....

....

Being sick makes me feel

....

....

....

....

Being tickled makes me feel

....

....

....

....

When we treat our bodies well – for example, by doing exercise, drinking a lot of water, or getting a good night's sleep – we can help to put ourselves in a *good* mood.

But if we treat our bodies badly – for example, by staying up too late, or eating too much, or forgetting our raincoat and getting wet – we will end up in a *bad* mood.

It's easy to forget how our bodies can influence our emotions. Sometimes, when we're in a particularly good or bad mood, we can be wrong about what has caused it. We might think we're angry because we can't find our shoes, or because our parents are being annoying – but it might really be because we're tired, or hungry or unwell.

Moods and Art

Another thing that affects our emotions is art. Artists create pieces of art – like paintings, music, books, films – to express emotions: to show how *they* feel, and to try to make us feel the same way. We can sometimes speak of artworks having a particular *mood*.

Music is closely linked with emotions. Music that sounds happy or joyful is usually in a *major* key, while music that sounds sad tends to be in a *minor* key. Composers (people who write music) have written songs to inspire particular emotions, like Ludwig van Beethoven's 'Ode to Joy', or Rezső Seress's 'Gloomy Sunday'.

→ Why not listen for yourself? Listen to the following songs (you can get an adult to play them on their phone or computer) and write down what emotion you think they are trying to express:

1 'Mr Blue Sky' by ELO

....

2 'Masters of War' by Bob Dylan

....

3 'When I'm Cleaning Windows' by George Formby

....

4 'Claire de Lune' by Claude Debussy

....

5 'Lilac Wine' by Nina Simone

....

The same is true of paintings. Painters chose particular colours and images to try and express different emotions.

→ What emotions do these paintings make you feel?

Edvard Munch, *Ashes*, 1894

Joaquin Sorolla, *Running Along the Beach*, 1908

Georgia O'Keeffe, *The White Flower*, 1932

Jean-Michel Basquiat, *Victor 25448*, 1987

A happy song?

....

A sad book?

....

An exciting film?

....

An angry song

....

A disgusting book?

....

A scary film?

....

We can use art to help us *change* or *complement* our mood. If we're feeling sad, we can try to change our mood by looking at, listening to, watching or reading something happy. Or we might *complement* our mood with art that is similarly sad.

We don't always have to change our mood to feel better – sometimes, knowing that other people have felt the same way as we do can be very comforting. It makes us feel less alone.

Mood Diary

Our mood is very changeable. We feel all sorts of different emotions over the course of the day – so many that it can be hard to keep track of them.

To understand just how often our mood changes, it can be useful to keep a mood diary.

Time	What I was doing
8am	
9am	
10am	
11am	
12pm	
1pm	
2pm	
3pm	
4pm	
5pm	
6pm	

→ Why not keep a mood diary for the day? Write down what you were doing and feeling during each hour of the day, from the time you woke up to the time you go to bed.

Were you surprised by how often your mood changed?

	How I felt

Mystery Moods

It's normally quite easy to tell what has caused our emotions. But sometimes, we can feel sad, or joyful, or frightened for *no reason*. Our moods are a mystery.

→ Have you ever felt an emotion for no reason?

What was the emotion?

....

When did you feel it?

....

What were you doing?

....

Mystery moods are important, particularly if they last a long time. Some are quite common – so much so that there are names for them.

Anxiety – If someone feels worried or scared all the time, but doesn't know why. They might struggle to sleep or sometimes feel dizzy and unable to breathe.*

Depression – If someone feels sad (or doesn't ever feel happy), but doesn't know why. They might struggle to get out of bed, or do things they normally find fun.

Conditions like anxiety and depression can be very harmful. They stop us from enjoying life and can lead us to do things that are damaging to ourselves and others.

In order to stop our unexplained moods from becoming something harmful, we need to try to solve the mystery. We need to become *emotional explorers*.

*This is sometimes called a panic attack.

Solving Our Mystery Moods

Solving our mystery moods isn't easy. There are several reasons why finding the cause of our emotions is hard.

Sometimes it's because the emotion is *unfamiliar*. We might be feeling a new emotion. Maybe there's a classmate who we used to find annoying but now find unusually interesting – we might be feeling desire for the first time.

Sometimes it's because we've *forgotten* the reason. We might forget we had a bad night's sleep and imagine we're angry with the whole world because it's a horrible place. It isn't. You're just lacking an hour's sleep!

Sometimes things happen that bring up *old* emotions. Maybe someone close to you always shouted if you got something wrong. Now at school, you get scared if a teacher seems in any way annoyed or upset with you.

→ See if you can come up with some possible explanations for your mystery mood.

Possible explanation 1

....

....

Possible explanation 2

....

....

Possible explanation 3

....

....

My Mood Journey Postcard

Now that you've explored your moods, it's time to fill out your postcard. Use this space to record some of the things you've learned about yourself and your moods in this chapter.

→ On this side, draw and colour in a picture of something you've explored (perhaps a piece of art that symbolises what you're feeling).

1 ....

....

....

2 ....

....

....

3 ....

....

....

→ On this side, write down the three most
important things you've learned during
the chapter.

Exploring My
Imagination

Exploring My Imagination

A lot of the time, when we think, we think about what *is*. What exists, in reality – like what we've had for lunch, or how much homework we've got to do.

But our minds possess a surprising ability – the ability to think about what is *not*:

✳ What is *impossible*
✳ What is *original* (what has never been done before)
✳ What *might* happen in the future
✳ What *could* have happened differently

We use our imagination all the time. Often we imagine without meaning to – or even realising that we *are* imagining...

Play

Young people are especially good at using their imagination. One way they do this is through **play.**

Most forms of play involve **pretending**, or **make-believe**. We might imagine that instead of a small person, we're actually an international spy, or a murderous pirate. Or that we're not in our back garden after all, but a tropical jungle, and that the stick we're holding is really a sword, or a magician's staff.

What's your favourite thing to pretend to be?

....

....

What's your favourite place to pretend to go?

....

....

Play is exercise for our imagination – just like running is exercise for our bodies. This is why play is just as important as work (despite what some grown-ups might say). It helps us develop our imagination.

Older people aren't usually as good at using their imagination. It isn't that imagination gets less powerful as we age, it's just that most older people don't make time to play. They think they are too busy, serious and grown-up. But this is a silly thing to think. Adults need to play just as much as children do (which is why it's a good idea to encourage them to play games and pretend with you).

→ Why don't you ask an adult how they would answer these questions?

→ What do you like to dress up as? Draw it below.

Creativity

When we use our imagination to *make* something, we are being **creative**.
There are lots of ways of being creative. We might:

Paint an egg

Make a drawing

Write a short story

Make a model out of clay

Write a song

Invent a dance

Do an impression

Decorate a cake

→ Which of these activities do you like to do best? Draw a circle around it.

Just like playing, being creative helps us exercise our imagination. The more things we create, the more we can train our imagination to grow more powerful.

We can be creative anywhere, though we might find there are some places where we are more creative than others. Some people find they are most creative when they're in the bath or the shower.

When do you feel most creative?

....

....

....

Where do you feel most creative?

....

....

....

Originality

Sometimes, our imagination can come up with something that has never been thought of before. This is called **inventing**, or being **original**.

→ Can you invent a new animal? Draw one below. You could try to make it out of bits of other animals (like the head of a lion and the body of a snake, for example).

The author Lewis Carroll wrote a poem called 'Jabberwocky', which he filled with neologisms – original words that he invented. Here is the first verse:

'Twas brillig, and the slithy toves
Did gyre and gimble in the wabe:
All mimsy were the borogoves,
And the mome raths outgrabe.

→ Can you spot the neologisms? Underline or circle them.

→ Why don't you make up some new words? Come up with three new words and write down what they mean.

New Word	Definition

Empathy

On page 15, we talked about the problem of knowing what other people are thinking and feeling. One solution to this problem is *empathy*. To *empathise* with someone means to understand their minds.

Empathy is an act of imagination. We're imagining what other people *might* be thinking and feeling.

If we've ever felt a particular emotion, like being scared or lonely, we can imagine how other people might feel in scary or lonely situations, like fighting in a war or being all alone in a hospital, even if we've never been in those situations ourselves.

And if we've had a particular experience, like being bullied or losing a parent, we can imagine how other people feel who've had a similar experience, even if they're not much like us in other ways.

→ Can you imagine what these people are feeling? Can you remember a time when you felt something similar?

Lots of people don't use their empathy in this way. They concentrate on the ways they are *different* to other people – like the fact they have a different skin colour, or live in a different country – and ignore the ways in which they are *similar*.

It's a good idea to practise empathising with people, particularly if they seem very different to ourselves. By using our imagination, we can identify things that make us similar, which means we'll be able to relate to them better.

Dreams

One place where we do a lot of imagining is in our dreams.

Dreams are mysterious things. No one really knows *why* we have them, but all of us do. It's as if when they're not distracted by the real world, our minds are free to imagine different ones.

In our dreams, our imagination is king. Unlike the real world, our dreams aren't governed by logic or laws (like time or gravity). Impossible things can happen. We might be able to fly, move objects with our minds, walk on the moon or play games with ghosts.

Can you remember what happened in your dreams last night?
Write down anything strange that you can remember happening.

....

....

Though they don't always make a lot of sense, dreams can be useful. They give us clues about important things we should be paying attention to in our real lives.

If we have a dream where something bad happens, it might be because we're worried about it happening in real life. (These are sometimes called *anxiety dreams*.)

What's the worst thing that's ever happened to you in a dream?

....

....

....

And if we have a dream where something *good* happens, it might be because we wish that thing might happen to us in the future.

What's the best thing that's ever happened to you in a dream?

....

....

....

It's a good idea to make a note of your dreams – doing so can help you discover things you're worried about, and also what you're wishing for.

What do your dreams suggest you might be worried about?

....

....

....

What do your dreams suggest you might be wishing for?

....

....

....

Art

Artists use imagination to create art. A good definition of art is that it does something *original* – something that has *never been done before*.

Novelists write *fiction* – they make up stories about people that don't exist and events that haven't happened. Actors use *imitation* – using their imagination to think about what it might be like to be someone else.

Certain painters – like Pablo Picasso, René Magritte or Dorothea Tanning – try to look at the world in a new way. They chose images or subjects that exist in reality – like musicians, men in bowler hats, or sunflowers – then used their imagination to paint them in a way they've never been seen before.

René Magritte, *Golconda*, 1953
Pablo Picasso, *Three Musicians*, 1921
Dorothea Tanning, *Eine Kleine Nachtmusik*, 1943

→ Why don't you try drawing like Picasso, Magritte or Tanning? Choose an object or person to draw, and then use your imagination to draw them in a way *no one has been drawn before.*

→ Give your picture a name.

→ If you had to choose, what kind of artist would you like to be?

Inventors and Inventions

Inventors use imagination to solve people's problems. They identify a problem people have, something no one has been able to help with before, and use their imagination to come up with a machine or a piece of technology that can solve it.

Here are some examples:

Inventor	Problem	Invention
Alexander Graham Bell	*People who live far apart can't talk to each other*	The Telephone (1876)
Josephine Cochran	*It takes a lot of time and effort to wash dishes by hand*	The Dishwasher (1886)
Maria Beasley	*People need a way to escape from sinking ships*	The Life Raft (1880)
Orville and Wilbur Wright	*Gliders are not very good if you have a destination in mind*	The Airplane (1903)
Mary Anderson	*It's hard to see out the car windshield when it's raining*	The Windshield Wiper (1903)
Lonnie Johnson	*It's hard to get enemies really wet in water fights*	The Super Soaker (1990)

If you use our imagination, *you* can become an inventor. First, you need to identify a problem. Then, you need to invent a solution.

→ Come up with six inventions. We've given you three problems to get you started, but you should choose three more problems of your own to solve.

Problem	Invention
Shoelaces keep coming undone	
Coats and umbrellas stay wet when it's been raining	
Cereal goes soggy in milk	

Utopias

Utopia is a Greek word that means 'no place'. It is a place that exists only in our imagination.

A lot is wrong with the real world. There are buildings that are ugly, or abandoned. There are people who are poor, unhealthy and starving. There are a host of societal problems, like crime, pollution, racism and addiction, which cause suffering and unhappiness.

That's why we need to think about utopias. We create a utopia by using our imagination to think of ways in which the world could be better than it is now, with more beautiful buildings, improved methods of transportation, and technological solutions to the problems of today.

→ These pictures were drawn more than fifty years ago, imagining what the world of the 21st century might (ideally) look like. Can you spot what they got right – and wrong?

This is a very important use of imagination. Creating utopias can help us think of ways in which our houses, towns and cities can be improved. We don't have to just accept the problems we live with and see all around us. By using our imagination, we can start to think about how, in the future, we might be able to solve them.

→ Create your own utopia. Draw the skyline of an ideal town or city. Use your imagination to think about how this city is better than the ones you are familiar with. What do the buildings look like? How do people get around? Is there a park with trees, or a swimming pool?

Why Imagination Can Be Bad

We've looked at some of the ways in which imagination can be helpful. But sometimes, it can be very *unhelpful* – principally, when we mistake imagination for reality.

Let's look at an example. Lots of people, particularly when they're young, are scared of the dark. They're not scared of darkness itself; they imagine that something dangerous or deadly might be hiding there, like a monster, or a burglar.

→ Draw something scary that you imagine might lurk in the dark.

But the truth is, it's very unlikely that what we imagine *could* be hiding in the darkness actually is. The reason we're scared is because we're mistaking our imagination for reality.

Another mistake we make is to think that things that *could* or *might* happen definitely *will* happen. One error that a lot of people make when they're worried about something (like a dentist appointment, or a test at school) is to imagine that the *worst possible thing* might happen. We imagine that the dentist will use horrible implements on our teeth, leaving us in great pain or disfigured, or that we'll be thrown out of school for being stupid, and that our parents will never forgive us. This is called *catastrophising*.

→ What's the worst thing you can imagine happening in the following situations?

Breaking something expensive in your house	Slipping on a patch of ice
Getting lost on the way home	Eating some out-of-date food

Again, it's very unlikely that the worst thing we can imagine will happen – and even if it did, in all probability we would be all right in the long run. When we're worried, we need to be aware of our capacity for imagination: doing so can help us realise that what we're worried about isn't actually very likely.

My Imagination Journey Postcard

Now that you've explored your imagination, it's time to fill out your postcard. Use this space to record some of the things you've learned about yourself and your imagination in this chapter.

→ On this side, draw and colour in a picture of something you've explored (maybe a picture of a creature you made up living in the utopia you created).

1 ....

....

....

2 ....

....

....

3 ....

....

....

→ On this side, write down the three most
important things you've learned during
the chapter.

Exploring My Conscience

What is My Conscience?

Your conscience is your sense of right and wrong. It's an **inner voice** that tells you what is a **moral** (good) or an **immoral** (bad) way to behave, and tries its best to persuade you to be good.

→ Here's a list of different ways you can behave. Listen to your conscience and sort them into what you think is either a moral or an immoral way to behave.

Stealing biscuits from
the cupboard

Helping someone
who's fallen over

Pretending to be ill to get
a day off school

Doing all your homework
on time

Sharing a snack with
someone

Cleaning up after yourself

Putting socks on
your pet

Spreading rumours about
a classmate

Drawing on the walls

Dropping rubbish
on the floor

Moral	Immoral

Though your conscience is just a part of your mind, some people have imagined that their conscience is a person or a creature. The ancient Greeks called them **daimons**.

→ If you could see your conscience, what would it look like? Use your imagination and draw your conscience here.

What is Right and Wrong?

How do we know what is right and wrong? It's a very good question. Philosophers have been arguing about it for thousands of years...*

Generally, when we say something is 'moral', we mean that it is *helpful*. It's an act, or a way of behaving, that helps people. It's something that brings them happiness, solves a problem they have, or soothes their pain.

(*There's a whole school of philosophy about this question called Ethics.)

We call something 'immoral' when it is *hurtful*. It's an act, or a way of behaving, that harms other people. It is something that makes them unhappy, or causes them difficulty or discomfort.

Of course, it's much nicer when people are helpful than when they are hurtful, so almost everyone prefers people to act morally rather than immorally.

Conscience Comics

→ What would your conscience tell you to do in these situations? Draw what you think is the immoral and the moral way to act.

Walking along…

Finding a wallet with money…

Immoral act

Moral act

Two friends buying ice creams...

One friend drops theirs...

Immoral act

Moral act

Conscience Comics…

Two girls enter a sweet shop…

One sees the other stuffing sweets into her bag…

Immoral act

Moral act

A boy walks down the corridor at school…

Turns a corner and sees one boy beating another up…

Immoral act

Moral act

Where Does Conscience Come From?

No one is born with a conscience. You'll notice babies don't care much about sharing or being quiet when someone else is talking. Instead, we learn what is right and wrong in two ways: from **teaching** and from our own **experience**.

Grown-ups spend a lot of time either praising or telling us off for the things we do. They're trying to develop our conscience by teaching us what is moral and what is immoral. Even if we sometimes find what they say annoying or embarrassing, we'll probably remember the things they say for the rest of our lives.

→ Here are some grown-ups you might know. Write down some of the things you remember them telling you about what is right and wrong.

Your parent or caregiver:

Your teacher:

We're also taught to act morally by **society**. In a society, people are governed by **laws**, which are rules that control their behaviour. Many immoral acts (like stealing, or hurting people) are criminalised, which means you can be punished or sent to prison for doing them.

Religions also teach what is right and wrong. Most religions instruct their followers on how to lead a moral life. They also use laws (a famous example being the Ten Commandments from the Christian Bible).

→ If you were in charge, what laws would you make? Write down three laws that you would institute if you were in charge.

Law 1

....

....

Law 2

....

....

Law 3

....

....

Experience

Our own individual sense of right and wrong also comes from our own experience.

When other people treat us in a way that we find helpful, we recognise that this is *good* or *moral* behaviour. When people treat us in a way that we find *hurtful* – for example, by making fun of us or calling us names behind our back – we call this *bad* or *immoral* behaviour.

→ Can you remember three different ways someone else has helped you? And three different ways someone else has hurt you?

Three ways people have helped me	Three ways people have hurt me

As we grow up, our experience of helpful and hurtful behaviour helps to develop our personal **morality.** We're following what is known as the **golden rule** of right and wrong:

→ Can you turn your six experiences into personal rules for how to treat others?

"Treat others as you would like others to treat you."

Rule 1

....

Rule 2

....

Rule 3

....

Rule 4

....

Rule 5

....

Rule 6

....

Why Should We Be Good?

Of course, it's much nicer when other people are helpful than when they are hurtful. But that's not the only reason to be good. Acting morally makes *us* feel better than acting immorally.

This is because humans are social animals. We *like* helping other people. It brings us a sense of **fulfilment,** which means that we feel good about ourselves. It could even be said that the **meaning of life** is to help others.

Because of this, there are grown-ups who make it their job to help others.

→ How do each of these people help others as part of their job?

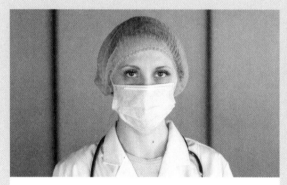

How they help people:

....

....

....

How they help people:

....

....

....

How they help people:

....

....

....

How they help people:

....

....

....

(Remember, helping people doesn't just mean keeping them safe or healthy. It can also mean bringing them happiness.) A lot of grown-ups are unhappy in their jobs. One of the biggest reasons for this is because they don't feel like their work does any good.

When thinking about what job you might like to have when you grow up, it's a good idea to start by thinking about how you might be able to help people, and choosing a job that allows you to do this.

A skill I have is

....

I can help people with this by

....

A job I might do is

....

Following Your Conscience

It's not always easy to listen to your conscience. Sometimes it can be very tempting to do the wrong thing.

A lot of things that are hurtful to others can benefit us in the short term. If we lie about who drew on the bedroom wall or spilt orange juice on the carpet, and let someone else take the blame, we benefit from not being in trouble, even as we're hurting someone else in the process.

→ Have you ever done the wrong thing? Write down the reasons you did it, and why it may have hurt someone else.

What I did wrong	How it benefited me	Why it was hurtful to others

Most of the time, people who act immorally are being selfish. They're putting their own needs above other people's. Acting morally involves doing the opposite: putting other people's needs above our own.

Ignoring our conscience might benefit us in the short term. But listening to our conscience and doing the right thing will benefit us in the longer term. Other people will like and trust us more, and we'll feel better about ourselves.

Guilt

Our conscience doesn't just tell us how we should act in the future. It also tells us what we should have done differently in the past.

If we do something that our conscience tells us is wrong, we might start to feel bad about it afterwards. This is called feeling **guilt** (or **remorse**).

→ Write down three things you've done that you feel guilty about – and what your conscience tells you that you should have done differently.

What I feel guilty about	What I should have done differently

Guilt can be very powerful. If we've done something particularly bad, we can feel guilty for a long time afterwards.

Of course, we can't change the past. Whenever we feel guilty, we should think of it as a lesson we've learned about how we should act in the future.

→ Look at the three things you feel guilty about on the previous page. Turn them into three lessons you should remember about how to act in the future.

Lesson 1

....

....

....

....

Lesson 2

....

....

....

....

Lesson 3

....

....

....

....

Moral Absolutes

We tend to think that there are set rules about what is right and wrong. But rules about what is right and wrong aren't always black and white.

Most people agree that telling lies is wrong. But there might be some occasions where lies are actually kinder than the truth. For example, if someone has given you a present that you don't really like, it might be kinder to pretend you *do* like it, rather than hurt their feelings by telling them you don't.

→ Can you think of some exceptions to these moral rules?

Rule	Exception (What if…)
Stealing is always wrong.	
Sharing is always right.	
Hurting people is always wrong.	

Similarly, if people do things that are wrong, there can be explanations as to why it is not completely their fault.

* They might be **ignorant** (for example, if they're very young or haven't been taught well).
* They might be **disadvantaged** (for example, if they were very poor or hungry).
* They might be **mentally unwell**.
* They might be **under duress** (which means someone else is forcing them to do it).

→ Can you think of some possible excuses for these types of behaviour? Use your empathy to see if you can come up with some explanations.

Immoral act	Explanation (What if...)
A child draws on their bedroom wall.	
A woman steals a loaf of bread from a supermarket.	
A man burns down his own house.	

When we see people doing wrong, we shouldn't always rush to judge or condemn them. We should also use our empathy to understand *why* they might be doing something we would consider wrong.

Punishment vs Forgiveness

None of us is perfect. All of us do the wrong thing from time to time.

Traditionally, the way we deal with people who've done wrong is **punishment**. Because they've hurt others, we do something hurtful to them – like sending them to their room, or locking them in prison – as **retribution**.

But another way is **forgiveness**. So long as they're willing to admit they've done wrong and **apologise**, we treat them with kindness and forgive them.

Forgiveness is a moral act. Instead of hurting someone who has hurt us, we choose to help them instead. Sometimes, forgiveness is more effective than punishment – because the person feels grateful, they're more likely to do good in the future than if they'd been punished.

It's not always easy to forgive, but often it's necessary. That's why we need to practise forgiving those who have hurt us.

→ Is there anyone who's hurt you who you would like to forgive? Write them a letter of forgiveness opposite. Why not copy this letter and send it to them? Everyone likes to be forgiven.

Dear

I would like to forgive you for

....

....

I found this hurtful because

....

....

But I understand you did it because

....

....

I still care about you because you are

....

....

I hope in future we can

....

....

From

Morals

As we mentioned earlier, morality isn't black and white. Our ideas about what is moral and immoral can change over time.

In the past, humans did many things that today we would consider very wrong, but which the majority of people at the time thought were perfectly okay.

But there were also people who recognised that these things were wrong even at the time. Some of them became **campaigners,** trying to convince others to see that they were wrong. Gradually, they convinced more and more people, so that these days, hardly anyone thinks that torture, child labour or slavery are acceptable.

If we explore our conscience, we might start to notice things that society accepts but that we think are wrong and should change.

→ Can you spot anything wrong in these pictures? What do you think should change?

What is wrong?

....

....

....

What should change?

....

....

....

What is wrong?

....

....

....

What should change?

....

....

....

This is a big reason why we should explore our conscience: so that, in future, we can help other people, and society as a whole, to do good.

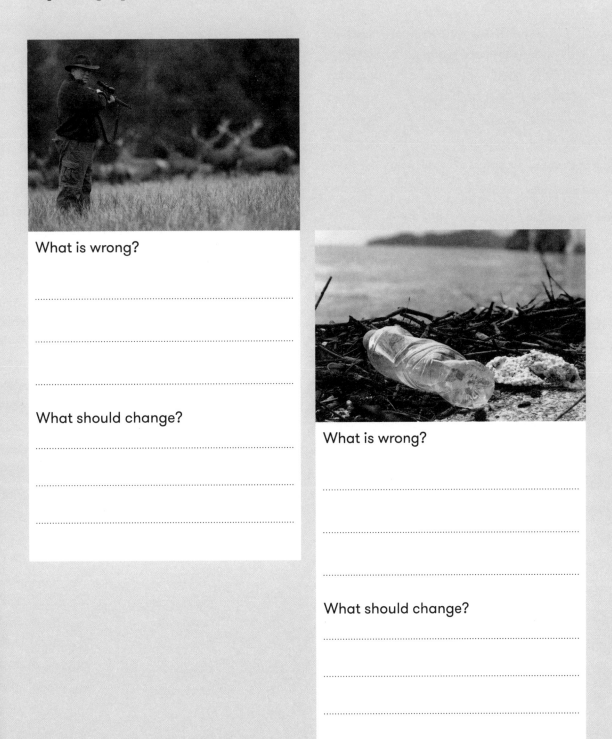

What is wrong?

....

....

....

What should change?

....

....

....

What is wrong?

....

....

....

What should change?

....

....

....

My Conscience Postcard

Now that you've explored your conscience, it's time to fill out your postcard. Use this space to record some of the things you've learned about yourself and your conscience in this chapter.

→ On this side, draw and colour in a picture of something you've explored (perhaps a moral or an immoral act you've done in the past).

1 ....

....

....

2 ....

....

....

3 ....

....

....

→ On this side, write down the three most important things you've learned during the chapter.

Exploring My Body

Exploring My Body

Your body is a pretty remarkable thing. It's made up of:

37 trillion cells

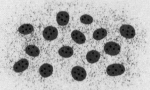

4–5 litres of blood

60,000 miles of blood vessels

7 trillion nerves

Around 250 different bones

1.7 square metres of skin

78 different organs

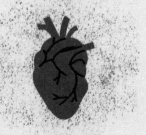

Bodies come in all different shapes and sizes. Some people are big, and others small. Some people have darker skin, and others lighter. Some people use their legs to get around, while others use a wheelchair.

Without your body, your self would not exist. But your body is not your *whole self*, as we shall see...

Physical Inventory

Your body probably feels pretty familiar – after all, you take it with you everywhere you go. But there's lots about your body that still remains a mystery.

→ Find out the following facts about your body. You'll need a ruler or a tape measure to help you.

I have _____ teeth.

My legs are _____ cm long.

My ears are _____ cm apart.

I have _____ lines on my palm.

My belly button is the size of a _____

My eyes are the same colour as _____

My hair is the same colour as _____

I can hold my breath for _____ seconds.

I can hum without stopping for _____ seconds.

Our bodies do strange things. Sometimes they make strange noises, like rumbles and gurgles. Sometimes bits of them tremble and ache for no reason.

→ What are three strange things your body does?

1. ....

....

2. ....

....

3. ....

....

Body Predictions

Our bodies are constantly changing. When we're young, it will grow an average of 2–5 inches taller each year. During **puberty**, it will grow hair and pimples in unexpected places. When we're old, the skin will wrinkle, and the muscles and bones will weaken. Certain bits of our bodies, like our ears and our nose, will keep on growing for our entire lives.

→ Draw what you think your body might look like in the future.

When I'm 20 years old

When I'm 40 years old

When I'm 60 years old

(If you keep hold of this book as
you grow older you'll be able to
check to see how accurate your
predictions were.)

When I'm 80 years old

Body Scrapbook

A scrapbook is a place to store pieces of history. Photographs, newspaper clippings, pressed leaves... anything that you can stick down on paper.

→ Why not start a scrapbook for your body? On this page, keep some mementos of your body's history by including:

A couple of hairs
(Pluck out and stick in with sticky tape)

A fingernail
(Clip off and stick in with sticky tape)

An eyelash
(Find a loose one and fix with sticky tape)

A fingerprint
(Dip in ink and smudge on page)

Bodily Sensations

The human body has many senses. You may have heard of the core five: **sight, sound, smell, taste** and **touch.**

→ Do you know what parts of your body are responsible for which sense? Draw lines to connect each sense to the correct organ (body part).

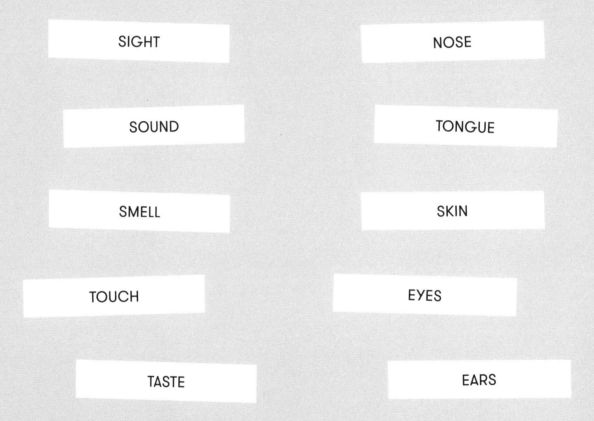

SIGHT	NOSE
SOUND	TONGUE
SMELL	SKIN
TOUCH	EYES
TASTE	EARS

Everything you've ever learned, or experienced, has come through your senses. Some sensations are pleasant, like tasting chocolate, or dipping your feet in cold water on a hot day. And some are unpleasant, like smelling dog poo, or listening to loud drilling.

→ What are your most and least favourite types of sensation?

My favourite sight is

....

....

My least favourite sight is

....

....

My favourite sound is

....

....

My least favourite sound is

....

....

My favourite smell is

....

....

My least favourite smell is

....

....

My favourite taste is

....

....

My least favourite taste is

....

....

My favourite thing to touch is

....

....

My least favourite thing to touch is

....

....

Disgusting Bodies

Your body does a lot of things that are sometimes called disgusting. It makes weird noises, unpleasant smells and yucky fluids.

→ What are three disgusting things your body does?

1 ....

2 ....

3 ....

Other people don't mind these things so much when we're babies. But as we grow older, we're encouraged to do them in private (usually on our own in the bathroom).

It's more polite to be disgusting in private. But sometimes we can start to feel ashamed of our bodies, thinking that we are disgusting because of what they do.

A very clever philosopher called Michel de Montaigne thought that we shouldn't be ashamed of the things our bodies do, because everybody does them (even if they pretend not to). As he reminded us:

"Kings and philosophers poo and so do ladies."

→ To help you remember this, draw the leader of your country (the king, queen, president or prime minister) having a poo.

Exercise

As you probably know by now, your body needs exercise. This means being **active** – running, skipping, jumping, stretching and moving about.

There are lots of different ways to exercise. We can exercise alone, by cycling, swimming or lifting weights. Or we can exercise with other people, by playing games, like hockey, football or badminton.

→ What are your three favourite ways to exercise?

1 ....

2 ....

3 ....

We're often told that exercise is good for our bodies – helping them to grow stronger and fitter. What's said less often is that exercise is good for our minds too. Exercise releases **endorphins**, chemicals in the brain that put us in a good mood. Exercise can stop us feeling sad, angry or worried, and help us feel joyful and hopeful instead.

→ Try this now. Write down how you're currently feeling, then again after 10–30 minutes of exercise.

How I felt *before* exercise: ....

How I felt *after* exercise: ....

This is why, even if you don't especially care about being strong or muscular, you should still exercise as often as possible.

Sex and Gender

Your **sex** refers to the kind of sexual organs your body has. Most people have either a **penis** or a **vagina** (although a very small number of people are **intersex,** which means they have a mixture of the two).

Your **gender** refers to your **identity** – whether you call yourself a **boy** or a **girl**. Most people with a penis identify as boys, and most with a vagina as girls – but not all.

What gender do you identify as? _____

In some societies, there are strict rules about gender. If we identify as a boy, we are supposed to only like so-called 'boyish' things, like toy soldiers or robots. And if we identify as a girl, we're supposed to only like so-called 'girly' things, like ballet or princesses.

But the truth is more complicated, we are all a mixture. We might like football, but also like playing with dolls. Or we might like wearing dresses, but also enjoy arm wrestling.

→ Make a list of the so-called 'girly' and 'boyish' things you do and don't like.

'Girly' things I like	'Girly' things I don't like
'Boyish' things I like	'Boyish' things I don't like

Disliking My Body

It's not unusual for people to dislike certain parts of their bodies. They might think their ears are too big, or their chin is too small, or their eyes are too close together. Some even have surgery to change the parts they dislike.

Is there a part of your body you dislike?

....

....

....

....

....

What don't you like about it?

....

....

....

....

....

But we shouldn't be too quick to try to change our bodies. If parts of us are unusual, they make us stand out. Being different to other people isn't a bad thing, particularly if we want to be famous.

After getting into a fight with a friend at school, the musician David Bowie was left with a permanently dilated pupil. It made him look quite unusual, helping him to stand out. He later thanked the friend for damaging his eye, which he said had helped to make him famous.

The singer and actor Barbra Streisand had a large nose with a bump in it. Though she was encouraged to get plastic surgery, she refused, saying: "I love my bump, I wouldn't get my bump cut off". Because there weren't many other singers or actors who had noses like hers, it became her trademark.

The model Winnie Harlow was born with a condition called vitiligo, which causes skin to lose its pigment and become pale in places. Looking different from other models helped to make her famous. She uses her platform to raise awareness of her condition.

We shouldn't dislike our oddities. They're what make us individual and give us character. They make us us.

Am I My Body?

Sadly, there will always be people who will judge us for what we look like. We can be judged for being short – or tall. We can be judged for being fat – or being skinny. We can be judged for having a particular skin colour, or accent, or ability.

Have you ever been judged for what you look like?

....

....

....

How did it make you feel?

....

....

....

It's important not to listen to these people. No type of body is better than any other. In the grand scheme of things, what your body looks like doesn't really matter.

What is more important is your character. It's who you are inside – not outside – that counts.

→ Write down three brilliant things about my body and character:

Brilliant things about my body	Brilliant things about my character
1	1 ....
....	....
....	....
2	2 ....
....	....
....	....
3	3 ....
....	....
....	....

My Body Journey Postcard

Now that you've explored your body, it's time to fill out your postcard. Use this space to record some of the things you've learned about yourself and your body in this chapter.

→ On this side, draw and colour in a picture of something you've explored (perhaps a self-portrait of your body).

1 ....

....

....

2 ....

....

....

3 ....

....

....

→ On this side, write down the three most
important things you've learned during
the chapter.

Exploring My Relationships

Exploring My Relationships

The poet John Donne once wrote:

What he meant is that none of us can exist without other people. We need **relationships** – to make connections with other human beings. We need to connect with our friends, our family, our classmates... and every so often, with someone we've never met before.

These relationships are a part of us. The people we choose to connect with, and the kinds of relationship we have with them, reveal a lot about who we really are.

Family

A family is a group of people who have something in common. They might be related by blood, or by marriage. They might live in the same house, or share the same name.

Families come in all shapes and sizes. We might have one parent, or three. We might have no siblings, or dozens. They can contain hundreds of people, or be as small as just two.

How many people are in your family? _____

→ Draw a portrait of your family below. Draw the person or people you are closest to in the centre, and those you are less close with towards the edge.

My Family Tree

A family tree is a record of our **biological** relations – our parents, grandparents, great-grandparents, great-great-grandparents, and so on...

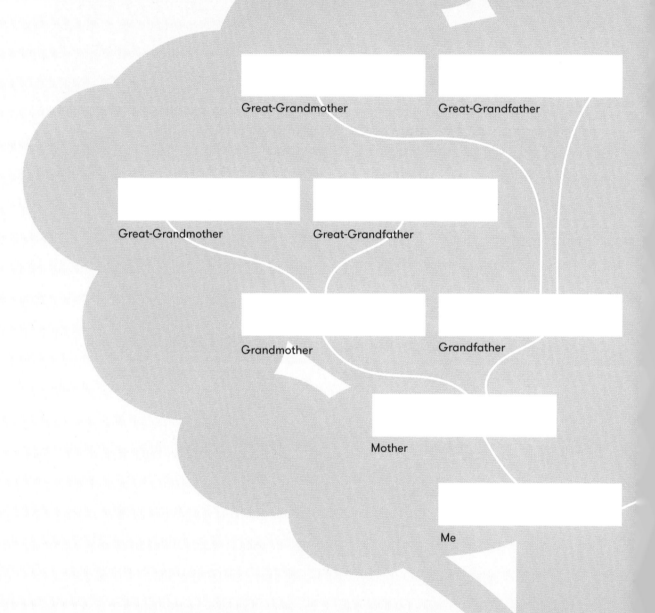

Great-Grandmother

Great-Grandfather

Great-Grandmother

Great-Grandfather

Grandmother

Grandfather

Mother

Me

→ See how much of this family tree you can complete. If you can, ask some of your relatives for help.

[ ]
Great-Grandmother

[ ]
Great-Grandfather

[ ]
Great-Grandmother

[ ]
Great-Grandfather

[ ]
Grandmother

[ ]
Grandfather

[ ]
Father

Don't worry if you can't complete all of it, or even some – in fact, that's very normal. Even if we don't know their names, we're descended from millions of different people. Our family tree is impossibly large.

Happy Families

Families, we're told, come in two different kinds. There are 'happy' families and 'unhappy' families.

Happy

Unhappy

The truth is more complicated. Families don't always get on, and can often be very cruel to one another. We can find other family members annoying, embarrassing, mean or unfair, and still love them.

Sometimes my

....

annoys me by

....

....

Sometimes my

....

embarrasses me by

....

....

Sometimes my

....

is mean to me by

....

....

Sometimes my

....

is unfair to me by

....

....

Families are neither happy nor unhappy – much of the time, they are both. They can be the cause of our greatest happiness, and our worst pains.

The best thing about my family is

....

The worst thing about my family is

....

Friendships

A friend is someone we have a deep connection with. They're someone we like, and who likes us in return.

→ My friends

1 ....

2 ....

3 ....

4 ....

5 ....

Friendships are very important – just as important as family. Unlike our family, our friends are **chosen**. The kinds of people we choose to be friends with reveal a lot about us.

My friends	What I like about them
....	....
....	....
....	....
....	....

Do you notice anything in common between what you like about your different friends?

Things I like about my friends in common

....

....

....

....

It shows the kinds of things you value in people (and in general).

How to Make Friends

It isn't always easy to make friends. Even if we have friends we're very close with, we can struggle to remember what it is that made us friends in the first place.

Friendships are built by **shared knowledge**. A friend is someone who knows us better than most other people. They understand parts of us that we might ordinarily keep secret, like the fact that we're scared of mice, or find it difficult to tie our shoelaces.

My friend	A secret I know about them	A secret they know about me

Sharing secrets about ourselves can be scary. We have to be brave enough to share information about ourselves that we wouldn't normally share, and to trust that they won't share it with other people. This is called being vulnerable.

What's a fact about yourself you would only share with a friend?

....

....

....

Sharing secrets about ourselves can be scary. We have to be brave enough to share information about ourselves that we wouldn't normally share, and to trust that they won't share it with other people. This is called being **vulnerable**.

We also have to be curious to find out things about people. We have to be good at listening and asking questions.

Here are some good questions you can ask new people to help turn them into friends:

"What are you scared of?"

"What rules do you like to break?"

"When do you feel lonely?"

"What don't people understand about you?"

Enemies

From time to time, we will have enemies. There will be people we don't like, and people who don't like us.

→ Do you have any enemies like this? Give an example of either (or both).

Someone I don't like:

....

Someone who doesn't like me:

....

Most enemies are made through **envy**. Envy is the unpleasant feeling we get when someone else has something we want very badly. They might be more popular than we are, or get the top mark in our favourite subject at school, or come from a richer family.

Who do you envy?

....

What do you envy about them?

....

Similarly, if someone doesn't like us, it might be because they envy us. If we get teased for being a teacher's pet, for example, the real reason might be because other people envy us for being smart.

What might someone else envy you for?

Envy can be difficult to deal with. But rather than focusing on the person we envy, we should think more closely about what we envy about them. Envy shows us things we secretly desire, even if we don't know it ourselves. It can be a guide to showing us what we want in our lives.

→ What are three things that you envy people for, that you might want more of in your life?

1

2

3

Shyness

Shyness is a feeling we sometimes get around strangers. We can get it at a party when we don't know many people, or when we go to a new country we've never been to before.

→ What situations do you feel shy in?

1 ....

2 ....

3 ....

Shyness comes from the idea that other people are very **different** to us. Because they seem different on the outside – because they are much older, or come from a different part of the world, or seem like they're cooler or more confident than we are – we assume they must be different on the inside as well. This makes us shy, because we think that we're too different to get on well.

→ Above each picture write down one way this person seems to different to you.

....

....

....

....

But you have much more in common with strangers than you realise. Inside, they're probably a lot like you. Everyone sometimes feels shy, or a bit stupid, or has things that scare them. The best way to cope with shyness is to think about what you might have in common with strangers.

→ Below each picture, write down something that you probably have in common with these people.

Loneliness

Loneliness is a feeling we get when we are disconnected from other people. Everyone gets lonely from time to time – even if we have lots of friends and a big family.

What makes you feel lonely?

....

....

We don't get lonely because we don't have enough relationships. It's because we don't have enough of the *right kinds* of relationship.

This is why you can be alone in your bedroom without feeling lonely at all, but feel very lonely when you're at a party with lots of other people, especially if you don't know them very well.

Not lonely

Lonely

To stop being lonely, we don't need to spend time with lots of different people. We just need to spend some time with the right kinds of people – the people who *understand* us.

What makes you feel the least lonely?

....

....

Other People

Our relationships will change over time. We will grow closer with some people, and more distant with others. Some of our relationships will end completely, and new ones will take their place.

Who's a new person you've met recently?

....

Who's a person you've grown more distant with?

....

Who's a person you've grown closer to?

....

Our relationships aren't just nice to have. They can teach us about ourselves. The more we understand other people – the things they like, the feelings they have, the problems they struggle with – the better we can understand ourselves.

My Relationships Journey Postcard

Now you've explored your relationships, it's time to fill out your postcard. Use this space to write down everything you've learned about yourself and your relationships from reading this chapter.

→ On this side, draw and colour in a picture of something you've explored (perhaps an image of you and your friends).

1 ....

....

....

2 ....

....

....

3 ....

....

....

→ On this side, write down the three most
important things you've learned during
the chapter.

Exploring My Hopes and Fears

Exploring My Hopes and Fears

Why do we *do* anything? There are things we *need* to do to survive, like eating, or keeping warm. But why do we do anything else?

We do things because there are also things we *want* – and things we don't. Each of us has **hopes** that we're trying to achieve, and **fears** we're trying to avoid.

We might not realise it – we might not even be *aware* we have them – but they can end up shaping our entire lives...

Favourite Things

→ What are some of your favourite things? Make a list of them here:

Colour?

....

Animal?

....

Food?

....

Drink?

....

Film?

....

Book?

....

Place?

....

School subject?

....

Day of the week?

....

Type of weather?

....

Season of the year?

....

Sound?

....

Smell?

....

Perfect Day

→ What would your perfect day look like? Plan out what you would do every hour.

Time	Activity
8am	
9am	
10am	
11am	
12pm	
1pm	
2pm	
3pm	
4pm	
5pm	
6pm	
7pm	

Goals

By thinking about our favourite things more closely, we can turn them into **goals**. A goal is something we want to achieve in life. Having goals gives our lives purpose – to achieve the goals we set for ourselves.

Let's say one of your favourite things to do is to play with Lego. If you were asked to say what it is you enjoy about it, you might say that you like working with your hands and using your creativity to design things. Knowing that you're the sort of person who enjoys this can help you start to think about what sort of job you might like when you grow up – like becoming an architect, for example, or a woodworker, or a designer.

One of my favourite things to do is

....

What I especially enjoy about it is

....

Therefore, I'm someone who likes

....

Therefore, a goal I might set myself is

....

Failure

Unfortunately, life doesn't always go to plan. There will be goals we want to achieve that we aren't able to, however hard we try.

→ Write down three things you've tried to do but been unable to:

1 ....

2 ....

3 ....

We don't tend to talk much about failure. We're much more likely to hear about success. We hear stories of award-winning actors, genius scientists and record-breaking sports stars.

But failure is very normal. Everyone fails at things. A 'successful' person isn't someone who has never failed. They're someone who's *learned* from their failures and kept going despite them.

We shouldn't be ashamed of our failures. Instead, we should see them as lessons. A mistake, misstep or setback is a guide to how to do things differently in the future.

Something I've failed to do	What the failure taught me
....	....
....	....
....	....

Scary Things

→ Write down ten things that scare you.

1

2

3

4

5

6

7

8

9

10

Why We Get Scared

In the past, life used to be very dangerous. Our distant ancestors faced lots of threats – like being attacked by wild animals or enemy tribes – that could easily be fatal. To stay safe, they had to be always on the lookout for danger. Being scared helped them to stay alive.

Life today is a lot less dangerous than it used to be. But our brains are still programmed to always be alert for danger, which means we still get scared of things (like creaky ceilings, or house spiders) that can't actually harm us.

We should never be ashamed of feeling scared – it's just the way our brains are programmed – but we should try to keep in mind how harmful it is.

→ Draw something you're scared of in your own life that the caveman is running away from.

Worrying

Worry is a response to fear. When we're worried about something (like finishing our homework on time), it's because we're scared of something particularly bad happening (like getting in trouble with our teacher and disappointing our parents).

→ Write down five things you worry about, and what you're scared of happening.

Something I worry about	What I'm scared might happen

Very often, the thing we're scared of happening isn't actually very likely to happen. This is because we're not usually using our reason, but our **imagination**. We're very good at imagining the worst possible thing happening, even if it's probably unlikely (this is called **catastrophising;** we talked about it on page 91).

How to Worry Less

Once we've worked out what we're scared of, we should ask ourselves two questions:

1.   How likely is it to happen?
2.   How harmful would it be?

Something I'm scared of	How likely is it to happen? (1–10)*	How harmful would it be? (1–10)**

*With 1 being 'virtually impossible' and 10 being 'very likely'
** With 1 being 'not harmful at all' and 10 being 'my life would be over'

You should notice that the numbers tend to be quite different. This is because when a bad thing is likely to happen, it probably isn't all that harmful. And when it is very harmful, it probably isn't likely to happen.

Resilience

Resilience is a kind of strength. It's not the same as physical strength. Instead, it's a kind of emotional strength.

Just as physical strength helps us overcome physical challenges (like lifting something heavy, or running for a long time), resilience helps us cope with emotional challenges (like failure). Someone who is very resilient can stay happy and hopeful even when bad things happen to them.

→ How resilient do you feel? Circle the number from 1 to 10

1	2	3	4	5	6	7	8	9	10

Not very
resilient

Very
resilient

Don't worry if you chose a low number – most people do. We're very bad at predicting how resilient we are. You've probably had things go wrong in your life that you've already overcome.

Something bad that's happened to me	How I overcame it
....	....
....	....
....	....
....	....

You should try to remember these things in future. When bad things happen, remember that you've overcome bad things in the past, and will do so in the future.

My Hopes and Fears Journey Postcard

Now that you've explored your hopes and fears, it's time to fill out your postcard. Use this space to record some of the things you've learned about yourself in this chapter.

→ On this side, draw and colour in a picture of something you've explored (perhaps one of your biggest hopes, or biggest fears).

1 ....

....

....

2 ....

....

....

3 ....

....

....

→ On this side, write down the three most
important things you've learned during
the chapter.

Conclusion

Conclusion

At the start of this book, we said that your self is like an undiscovered country. Now you've discovered a bit more about it, it's time to give yourself a flag.

Countries use flags to show their identity. The different colours and symbols are used to represent things that are important to that country.

Flag of Ghana

The red represents the blood of the forefathers.
The yellow represents the wealth of the country.
The green represents the country's forests.
The black star represents the freedom of the African people.

Flag of The Bahamas

The blue represents the blue seas.
The gold represents the golden sands.
The black triangle represents the strength of the people.

→ Design your own flag. Use colours and symbols to represent the things that are most important to you, and explain their meanings underneath.

....

....

....

....

....

....

The End?

This book has tried to take you a journey out of **self-ignorance** and towards **self-knowledge**. But though you've reached the end of the book, you haven't reached the end of your journey. In fact, you've only just begun.

When you started this book, you were here:

And now you've finished it, you're probably somewhere around here:

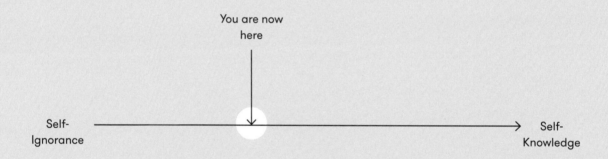

This might seem a little disappointing, but it shouldn't. Knowing yourself isn't something you can do in an afternoon, or a week, or a year. It takes an entire lifetime – and even then, you'll never *quite* be done.

This is because our self is always changing. Almost everything about us – our brains, our bodies, our behaviour, the friends we have and the things we like and dislike – will go on changing for the rest of our lives. (You've probably changed a little bit just in the time it's taken to complete this book.)

This doesn't mean we should give up on self-knowledge. It just means that we have to keep working at it. We'd encourage you to take a little bit of time to check in with your thoughts on a regular basis – spending five minutes a week doing some philosophical meditation is a good place to start. If you're interested in reading more or trying other exercises, The School of Life has other books and tools for both children and adults that can help you explore further.

You won't ever fully know yourself. But taking the time to get to know yourself a little better will help to make you happier, healthier and wiser.

Picture credits

p. 11   Heinrich Bünting, The entire world in the shape of a clover leaf, 1581 / Wikimedia Commons

p. 11   Antiquarian Images / Alamy Stock Photo

p. 12   Ian Dagnall / Alamy Stock Photo

p. 34   William Hogarth, *The Interior of Bedlam* from *A Rake's Progress*, 1735 (reissued 1763). Etching and engraving, 35.4 cm x 40.9 cm. The Metropolitan Museum of Art, New York, USA. Gift of Sarah Lazarus, 1891. SOTK2011 / Alamy Stock Photo

p. 59   Edvard Munch, *Ashes*, 1894. Oil on canvas, 120.5 cm x 141 cm. National Gallery of Norway, Oslo, Norway / Wikimedia Commons

p. 59   Joaquín Sorolla, *Running Along the Beach* [detail], 1908. Oil on canvas, Museo de Bellas Artes de Asturias, Oviedo, Spain / Wikimedia Commons

p. 59   Georgia O'Keeffe, *The White Flower*, 1932. Oil on canvas, 75.6 cm x 100.9 cm. Gift of Mrs. Inez Grant Parker in memory of Earle W. Grant / Bridgeman Images. © Georgia O'Keeffe Museum / DACS 2021

p. 59   Jean-Michel Basquiat, *Victor 25448*, 1987. Acrylic, oil stick, wax and crayon on paper laid on canvas, 182.9 cm x 332.7 cm. Photo: Christie's Images / Bridgeman Images. © The Estate of Jean-Michel Basquiat / ADAGP, Paris and DACS, London 2021

p. 78   Photo by Chalmers Butterfield / Wikimedia Commons (CC BY 2.5)

p. 78   Pormezz / Shutterstock

p. 79   SpeedKingz / Shutterstock

p. 79   BSIP SA / Alamy Stock Photo

p. 82   Pablo Picasso, *Three Musicians*, 1921. Oil on canvas, 200.7 cm x 222.9 cm. The Museum of Modern Art, New York, USA. Mrs. Simon Guggenheim Fund. © Succession Picasso / DACS, London 2021

p. 82   René Magritte, *Golconda (Golconde)*, 1953. Oil on canvas, 81 cm × 100 cm. The Menil Collection, Houston, USA. © ADAGP, Paris and DACS, London 2021

p. 82   Dorothea Tanning, *Eine Kleine Nachtmusik*, 1943. Oil on canvas, 41 cm x 61 cm. The Tate, London, England. Purchased with assistance from The Art Fund and the American Fund for the Tate Gallery 1997. © Photo Tate. © ADAGP, Paris and DACS, London 2021

p. 86   darkday / Flickr

p. 86   Andrey_Popov / Shutterstock

p. 86   Daniel Moqvist / Unsplash

p. 87   Klaus Bürgle, *The New Universe 85*, 1968.

p. 87   Forrest J. Ackerman Collection / CORBIS / Getty Images

p. 110   Bermix Studio / Unsplash

p. 110   Daniel Tausis / Unsplash

p. 111   nappy / Pexels

p. 111   Kay Roxby / Alamy Stock Photo

p. 120   De Luan / Alamy Stock Photo

p. 120   U.S. National Archives and Records Administration / Wikimedia Commons

p. 120   Hulton Archive / Stringer / Getty Images

p. 122   Followtheflow / Shutterstock

p. 122   Havillah / Shutterstock

p. 123   Canon Boy / Shutterstock

p. 123   Catherine Sheila / Pexels

p. 141   Christian Simonpietri / Sygma / VCG / Getty Images

p. 141   Bettmann / Contributor / Getty Images

p. 141   George Pimentel / Contributor / Getty Images

p. 161   Jorg Karg / Unsplash

p. 161   muroPhotographer / Shutterstock

p. 161   Rawpixel.com / Shutterstock

p. 186   Julinzy / Shutterstock

p. 186   Bahamas government / Wikimedia Commons

The School of Life tries to teach you everything you need to have a good life that they forget to teach you at school. We have shops all around the world, we run a YouTube channel and we have written a lot of books specifically for younger people, including books about philosophy, art, architecture, nature and the best way to have a healthy and happy mind.

theschooloflife.com